MW00975317

CHRISTMAS

Sue Carabine

Illustrations by

Shauna Mooney Kawasaki

Gibbs Smith, Publisher

First Edition
06 05 04 03 02   5 4 3 2 1

Text and illustrations © 2002 by Gibbs Smith, Publisher

Published by
Gibbs Smith, Publisher
P.O. Box 667
Layton, Utah 84041

Orders: (1-800) 748-5439
www.gibbs-smith.com

Designed and produced by
   Mary Ellen Thompson, TTA Designs
Printed in China

ISBN 1-58685-166-7

'Twas the night before Christmas
as Mom lay asleep—
The house still and quiet,
not even a peep.

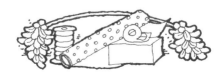

She woke with a start, cried,
"How long have I slept?"
Then looked at the time
and just about wept!

She remembered last night
getting home very late
'Cause things at the office
were in quite a state.

Their business had tripled
because of the season,
So no one left early,
no matter the reason.

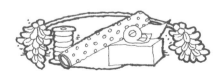

She'd rushed in the house
with a list on her mind—
If she started right now,
she'd not get behind.

So all of these thoughts
Mom wrote down on her list
To make certain each task
was completed, none missed.

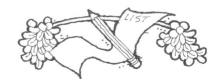

The rolls and the cookies
for Emily's school play,
First she would bake,
get that out of the way.

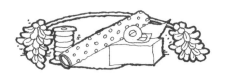

Then pies for the dinner—
apple, pumpkin and peach.
Something light Christmas Eve,
perhaps a nice quiche!

But before all the baking,

Meg's dress should be sewn,

The dance was at eight

(she'd let out a loud moan).

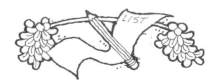

Just thinking about it
had made her depressed,
As she also must clean up
the house for the guests.

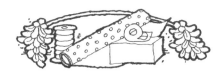

The bathrooms and kitchen
needed scrubbing for sure,
'Cause Aunt Nellie, she knew,
would insist on a tour!

If bedsheets were changed
and the vacuuming done,
Then trimming the tree and
the house might be fun.

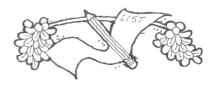

But the gifts must be wrapped,
and done so with care,
And the ones for the youngsters
hidden under the stairs!

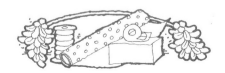

The treats for the neighbors
and friends must be planned,
Then carefully carried
and delivered by hand.

And last on her list,
she knew she'd be hopping
To catch the stores open
for last-minute shopping!

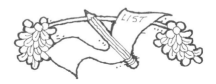

She'd laid down a moment
to take a short doze,
And then, she remembered,
her eyelids had closed.

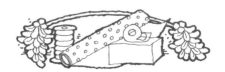

Now, as she sat up and
rubbed hard at her eyes,
She heard a sweet voice
whisper softly, "Surprise!"

Her family stood there
(they were all wide awake),
And the grins on their faces
almost made her heart break.

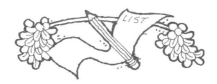

"Tell me again, please,
how long did I sleep?"
"About twenty-four hours,"
said Meg, at her feet.

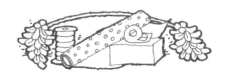

"Oh, my goodness, how could I?"
Mom cried with a tear,
"It looks like we'll have to
forget Christmas this year!"

"Oh, no, we won't, Mom,"
Nate leaped on the bed.
"Can I tell her, please, Daddy?"
the five-year-old said.

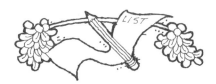

Dad chuckled and smiled,
"Well, I don't see why not
Since Santa and you, Nate,
came up with the plot!"

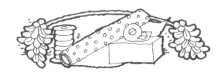

"Came up with what plot?"
Mom sounded upset.
"It's the night before Christmas
and nothing's done yet!"

Dad pulled Mother close,
saying, "Please, dear, relax.
Our Nathan will answer
the questions you've asked."

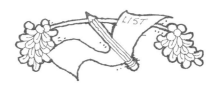

"When I came home, Mom,
and crept into your room,
I saw you asleep and
thought you'd wake up soon.

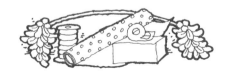

"But I waited and waited
and you didn't stir
So I telephoned Grandma
and explained it to her.

"She quickly came over,
we read your list through,
Then went to see Santa,
who knew what to do!

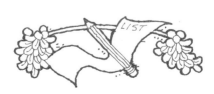

"I climbed on his knee,
whispered into his ear.
He grinned, 'This one's easy,
Nate, I'm glad you're here!'

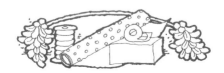

"Santa's eyes twinkled
as he went through the plan.
Then he said, 'Do you think
you can do that, young man?'

"I told him, 'I will,
with my family's help, too—
*And, please, Nick, remember
what I'd like from you.'*"

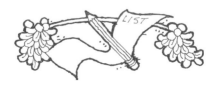

Well, Mom hid a smile
at Nate's hopeful remark,
Then worried 'bout getting
things done before dark.

But right at that moment
Emily rushed in the room,
And whispered to Dad,
"Is Mom coming down soon?"

Then Dad took Mom's arm
and they all walked downstairs
Where a beautiful sight
caught their Mom unawares.

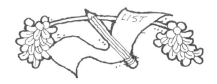

Hearing soft Christmas strains
(it was "O Holy Night"),
She looked up amazed,
saw her home filled with light!

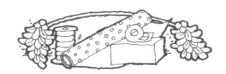

The Christmas tree sparkled,
the gifts were all wrapped,
And treats for the neighbors
were done while Mom napped.

From the kitchen Mom noticed
a wonderful smell,
And worries 'bout baking
were gone, she could tell.

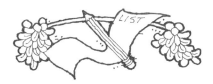

But, then she looked up
and cried, "Meggie, your dress!
I'm so sorry, my dear,
I slept too long, I guess."

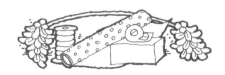

Meg slipped off her robe
and then twirled around fast.
"I sewed it myself, Mom.
The dance was a blast!"

With a lump in her throat,
Mom said, "How can this be?"
Her face full of wonder
at all she could see!

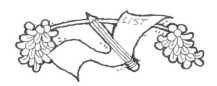

Her mind teemed with questions,
but what could she say?
How was her work finished—
and all in one day?

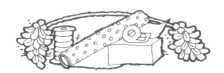

As if Dad knew her thoughts,
he laughingly said,
"Well, Emily and Meggie
cleaned bathrooms, changed beds.

"They polished and scrubbed
until everything glowed.
Then Em decorated,
Meg patiently sewed,

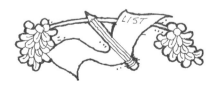

"While Grandma took Nathan
and followed your list.
They did all the shopping—
not one thing was missed.

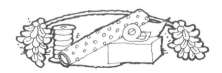

"As for me, you'll be proud
when you see all I've baked:
The pies and the cookies—
and even a cake!

"The quiche was a challenge,
as you will find out,
But we can always eat pizza
if you have any doubt."

Mom threw her head back
and laughed till she cried,
"My wonderful family,
you fill me with pride!

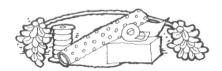

"The house looks so lovely,
I could not have done better.
I must write to thank Santa
and leave him my letter.

"The love that you've shown
I will never forget,
and know this will be
the very best Christmas yet!"

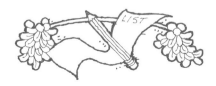

That night, eating cookies
and milk, St. Nick smiled
As he read Mom's sweet note
and just rested awhile.

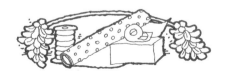

Then Nick called to Mom
as his reindeer took flight:
"YOU'RE the spirit of Christmas,
dear Mother, good night!"